W9-CVA-890

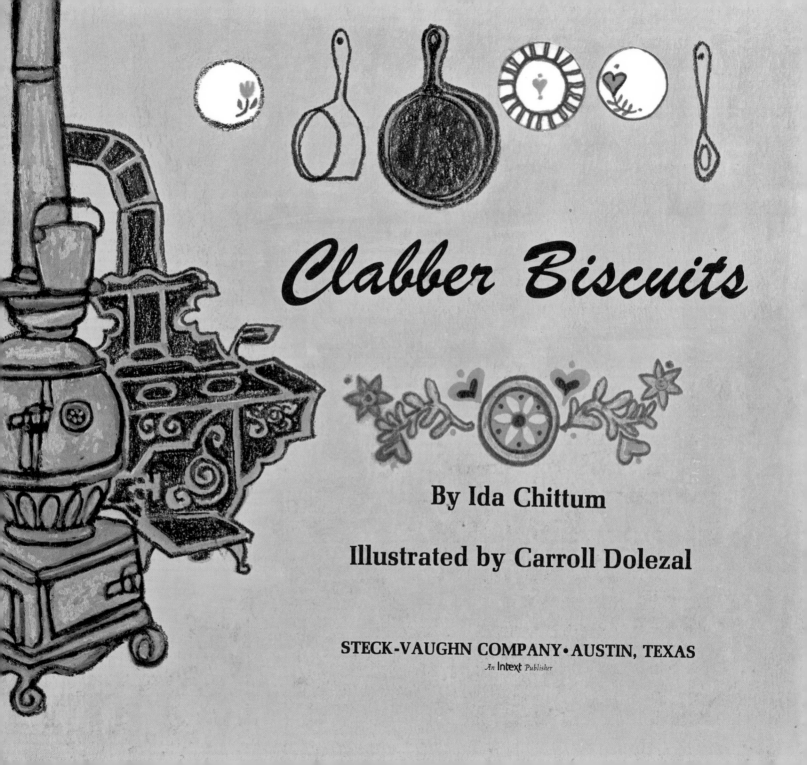

# Clabber Biscuits

## By Ida Chittum

## Illustrated by Carroll Dolezal

STECK-VAUGHN COMPANY • AUSTIN, TEXAS

An Intext Publisher

Library of Congress Cataloging in Publication Data

Chittum, Ida.
    Clabber biscuits.
    SUMMARY: Farmer Grit finally stops trying to bake the biscuits that are his wife's specialty and concocts something that will help her get well.
    I. Dolezal, Carroll, illus.    II. Title.
PZ7.C4453Cl        [E]        72-000077
ISBN 0-8114-7745-2

ISBN 0-8114-7745-2
Library of Congress Catalog Card Number 72-000077
Copyright © 1972 by Steck-Vaughn Company, Austin, Texas
All Rights Reserved

Printed and Bound in the United States of America

"I hurt here." Mama Grit clasped her back.
"I hurt there." Mama Grit thumped her head.
"It only hurts when I cook," she said and took
to her bed.

3

Flinging himself upon his knees, Farmer Grit
wept. "Without your tender clabber milk biscuits
we will all starve!" he cried.

The Grit twins, Joy and Solomon, heard all the
commotion and peeped from behind the kitchen door.

Mama Grit moaned louder and louder.

Farmer Grit's faithful coon hound Git howled
beside the kitchen stove.

The chickens clucked sadly from the stoop.

5

The donkey brayed from the field.

The ducks quacked mournfully. On their wide, wet, orange feet, they made the pilgrimage to the kitchen door.

"Where is our share of Mama Grit's tender clabber milk biscuits?" they quacked. Forty-eight orange-rimmed eyes stared pitifully at Farmer Grit. The air quivered with the thunderous sorrow of their quacks.

"Quiet!" Farmer Grit bellowed, for he was a bundle of nerves. "I'll mix you a batch of Mama Grit's tender clabber milk biscuits myself!"

"I have tasted your tender clabber milk biscuits before," howled Git. "Clabber they may be. Tender they are not. They are hard as rocks and twice as tasteless!" And Farmer Grit's faithful coon hound Git slunk off.

8

But Joy and Solomon thought biscuit making was a wonderful idea. "Hurrah!" they cried and ran to get Mama Grit's great cooking apron.

"The first step in biscuit making is the flour!"
said Farmer Grit, putting on the apron. He measured
the flour with a flourish. He stirred the mixing bowl
with such vigor that white clouds of flour floated
out the kitchen door.

10

The neighbors came on the run. "What is happening?" they cried.

"Mama Grit has taken to her bed. I am forced to make the clabber milk biscuits to keep us all fed," wailed Farmer Grit.

"It is a catastrophe!" the neighbors shouted.

"Bah!" cried Farmer Grit. "Bring me a crock
of clabber milk from the cellar," he called, flinging
an extra log into the fire. Smoke puffed up
from the cracks in the stove.

Farmer Grit rolled out the thick dough. "There, by jiggety," he cried. And he thrust a great pan of clabber biscuits into the oven. Then he fanned the fumes, soot, and smoke with his hat.

13

When Farmer Grit drew the cooked biscuits
from the oven, he tossed a generous batch
out the door to the waiting ducks.

"Who threw those rocks?" squawked the ducks as the biscuits banged their heads and sent them spinning.

"The first batch never turns out," said Farmer Grit.

"He forgot the baking soda," called out Joy. "The next batch will float right out the door."

15

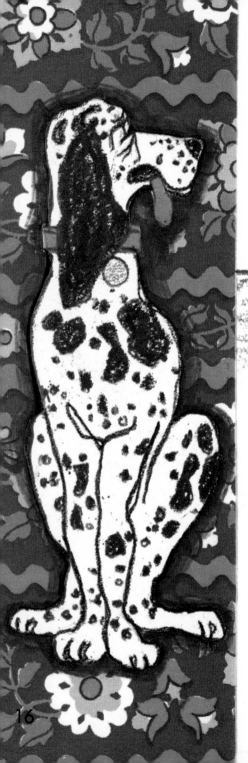

"It will never happen," yapped Farmer Grit's faithful coon dog Git.

And it never did. Each new batch of Farmer Grit's biscuits was harder than the last.

"Joy and Solomon, take the biscuits and edge the
flower bed of Mama Grit's petunias," Farmer Grit said,
for he wasn't a wasteful man. Then he warmed a
poultice of leaves, honey, and hog lard for Mama Grit.
He mixed a bowl full of sorghum molasses and sulfur.
He brewed spicebush tea.

But the sight of all of these made Mama Grit groan
all the louder.

"I still hurt here." Mama Grit clasped her back.
"I still hurt there." Mama Grit thumped her head.

18

In sympathy, the cow mooed. The goat baaed. The donkey brayed.

"Will she live?" the neighbors whispered.

Farmer Grit began running frantically about the cottage.

"What is he doing?" asked the nosiest neighbor.

"Is he counting eggs to sell to the grocer?" another asked.

"Is he bunching sassafras roots to sell to Mrs. Wiggins for her sassafras magic mixture?" an old man asked.

20

Farmer Grit didn't answer them. "This will cost money, but I will cure Mama Grit," he called to the twins. Then he dashed to the barn. He harnessed the horse to the buggy.

"He is going for the doctor." "He is going for his sister."
"He is going for her sister," shouted everyone all together.

"He has slicked his hair. He has changed his overalls.
Farmer Grit is a desperate man," the village scissor-
grinder said.

With one great leap, Farmer Grit was in the buggy.
With a loud crack, his shirttails flying, he flapped
the reins over the old mare's back. "Giddy-up!" he
shouted and was off in a cloud of dust.

"Will he get back in time?" the neighbors whispered.
They clung to each other fearfully, tongues clacking.

Back came Farmer Grit, thundering from the village.
He leaped from the buggy. A large box was in his arms.
He ran into the house. Joy and Solomon came running
after him.

A glad cry arose from the cottage.

24

The neighbors peered in the door and crowded around the windows.

"See Mama Grit in front of the cooking stove," one yelled. "Her tender clabber biscuit mixing bowl is in her arms."

25

Farmer Grit came to the door. "When tears, bitters, poultice, sorghum molasses, spice tea, and all else fails, my cure-all will do the trick every time!" he announced.

26

"Hurrah!" shouted the happy neighbors, throwing hats and aprons into the air.

The ducks quacked happily. The donkey brayed with delight.
The goat baaed hopefully. The twins jumped up and down
with glee.

"Gather round," Farmer Grit called to everyone. "We will have a tender clabber milk biscuit party!"

And they did. Mama Grit slapped platter after platter before the happy neighbors.

31

She wore Farmer Grit's cure-all, a spanking new
straw bonnet with a red, red rose swaying from the crown.